First published in 1976 by
JUPITER BOOKS (LONDON) LIMITED
167 Hermitage Road, London N4 1LZ

SBN 904041 522

Composed on the Monophoto in 16/20pt Bembo 270
by Art Reprographic (London) Limited, London
Printed in Great Britain by
C. J. Mason and Sons Limited, Bristol.

The Woolly Rhino
MEETS THE
WOOLLY MAMMOTH

Annabel Ogilvie *wrote the story*

T. A. B. Renton *drew the pictures*

JUPITER BOOKS

OR AS LONG AS THE Woolly Rhino could remember (which was not very long for the memories of Woolly Rhinos are rather short) the sun had shone daily on the mountains, plains and forests of his homeland. The Pterodactyls plummeted through clear blue skies, the Brontosauruses basked in their warm, deep pools and the Tyrannosauruses trundled across baking deserts. But though his friends seemed quite happy with the sunshine (including Fly whose favourite pastime was sun-bathing), the Woolly Rhino often felt his thick fur coat was not exactly suited to the warm weather.

One morning the Woolly Rhino woke suddenly to find Fly jumping up and down on his horn. 'Whatever is it?' he inquired sleepily. 'It can't be morning yet, Fly, the sun's not even up!' 'That's just it!' squeaked Fly excitedly. 'It's very light, but the sun isn't out and the sky is full of great fluffy grey . . . *things*!' (She meant clouds of course – but never having seen them before, she had no idea what they were called.)

'How very strange,' said the Woolly Rhino, who was still too sleepy to take much interest in the peculiar state of the weather.

'And that's not all,' Fly continued, quite determined to arouse the Woolly Rhino's interest. 'It actually feels rather cold!'

Cold? the Woolly Rhino thought. Cold? He was so fascinated by the suggestion that he forced himself to his feet and wandered outside to investigate.

Fly was quite right. Although he felt far from cold in his woolly coat, he did notice that it was definitely not as hot as usual.

Fly, to keep warm, was frantically beating her wings up and down and staring enviously at the Woolly Rhino's thick fur coat.

'It's all right for you,' she complained. 'You don't feel the the cold – you've got a warmer, woollier coat than everybody else!'

'Not quite everybody,' said a warm, rumbling voice from somewhere behind them.

Fly was startled and shot several feet into the air and the Woolly Rhino spun around on one foot, like a top. Standing looking at them was an animal with such an enormous thick coat of shaggy fur that the Woolly Rhino seemed almost bald in comparison. Beneath the creature's magnificent mane two large shining eyes peered out at them with a friendly gleam, while a wide smiling mouth showed two huge tusks which curved up and around and down to where his trailing fur met the ground.

'Who are you?' buzzed Fly inquisitively.

'Yes,' echoed the Woolly Rhino, 'who are you? You have even more hair than me!'

'My, my,' said the strange creature in his rich voice. 'Don't you youngsters know anything? I realise I haven't been here for quite sometime – but surely *someone* must remember me?'

The creature looked reproachfully at them through his long silky lashes and settled himself, quite uninvited, beside the entrance of their hollow-tree home.

The Woolly Rhino and Fly, who had noticed the drop in temperature since the creature's arrival, looked at him in amazement.

'I'm very sorry, Sir,' said the Woolly Rhino most politely. 'But who are you?'

'I,' said the creature with great pride, 'I am the Woolly Mammoth. The bringer of winter. When I come the sun leaves and takes her warmth elsewhere. I bring with me dancing snowflakes and the cold, gleaming beauty of frozen pools and pointed icicles. When I arrive many animals hide and sleep through the beauty of winter, while others put on their warmest coats and play in a crisp, ice-blue world quite different from the hot world of summer!'

The air around had become much colder as the Mammoth spoke and the sky filled with spinning white flakes. Soon the ground was covered in a thick white carpet which reached up as far as the Woolly Rhino's knees, and stretched out into the distance as far as Fly could see.

'Snow!' yelled the Woolly Rhino at the top of his voice. 'Snow! Snow! Snow!' And he jumped up and down clicking his heels together, and then ran off, kicking great clouds of snow into the air, trying to catch the falling snowflakes in his mouth.

'Well,' said Fly, who had fallen off the Woolly Rhino's horn when he had first jumped into the air. 'Just fancy that!'

'Never mind, Fly,' said the Woolly Mammoth kindly. 'Come and sit in my fur and keep warm and I'll explain it all to you.'

So as the Woolly Rhino chased snowflakes up and down a desert which had suddenly changed into a gleaming white wilderness, Fly flew over and sank happily into the thick fur of the Woolly Mammoth, from where she peeked out at the strange world around them.

'Now,' said the Woolly Mammoth in his deep, comfortable voice, 'I'll tell you all about Woolly Rhinos.' And he began to recite a poem:

They will glow
in the snow
for that's where they go
to be born and to grow
in the place where they live.

They're like mice
on the ice –
need I tell you twice?
They think winter's nice
in the place where they live.

They unfold
in the cold –
the young and the old
are happy and bold
in the place where they live.

And should one depart
from where its life starts
winter's dear to its heart
for it still is a part
of the place where it lived.

So your Woolly friend
can quite comprehend
how to mingle and blend
as the snowflakes descend
on this land where you live.

'But why does he live here then?' asked Fly. 'Usually
the sun shines all day, and although he gets a little hot
sometimes he seems quite happy.'

'He *is* quite happy, Fly,' agreed the Woolly Mammoth.
'When Woolly Rhinos leave their wintery homeland they
soon forget about it when they settle down elsewhere. It is
just that when I am here, bringing the cold with me, your
friend realises how lovely winter is.'

'Winter? Lovely? I'll have to think about that!' said Fly as she soared through the air towards the hollow-tree home she shared with the Woolly Rhino and disappeared indoors.

Meanwhile the Woolly Rhino was still happily chasing snowflakes – an energetic pursuit for a rather overweight Woolly Rhino who usually took very little in the way of exercise.

Suddenly his feet slid from under him and he skidded across a large patch of ice in a most undignified fashion. He came to a halt, with a bump, against a large grey object half-submerged in the ice.

'Ouch!' said an indignant voice far above his head, and the Woolly Rhino sat up with some difficulty and there, far above his head, towered a Brontosaurus who blinked down angrily at him.

'I would have thought,' the Brontosaurus said, 'that it was misfortune enough being frozen in the middle of my pond without having Woolly Rhinos skating across and bumping into me!'

'I'm awfully sorry . . .' the Woolly Rhino began, but he was interrupted by something wet and white hitting him in the back of the head and causing him to lose his balance and fall inelegantly onto the ice again. Hearing loud shouts of laughter from behind, the Woolly Rhino turned to see two young Tyrannosauruses standing on the edge of the pond.

'A Brontosaurus frozen in a pond and a Woolly Rhino who can't stand on his feet!' said one of them. 'The two of you make perfect targets for our snowballs!'

So saying, the Tyrannosauruses began hurling snowballs from a large pile, their aim improving with every throw.

One carefully-aimed snowball hit the Brontosaurus on her forehead and slid, icily, past her snout and all the way down her back.

'Really!' said the Brontosaurus shivering. 'This is too much!' And baring her teeth with effort and bracing her shoulders she pushed upwards until the ice shattered into a million small pieces. She was free!

Seeing the Brontosaurus's fierce expression and not wishing to continue their game now that she was free the two Tyrannosauruses each threw one last snowball for luck, and then raced away, giggling and shouting, through the snow.

Meanwhile the Woolly Rhino was floundering in the icy water, trying desperately to crawl out towards the bank.

'Help! Help!'

The Brontosaurus, who had been staring furiously at the Tyrannosauruses had forgotten all about the Woolly Rhino. She heard a faint squeak from somewhere behind her and turned to see the Woolly Rhino thrashing about in the cold, cold water.

'P-P-P-Please get m-m-m-me out!' pleaded the Woolly Rhino. 'P-P-P-please!' And his teeth chattered like castanets.

The Brontosaurus – who was really quite fond of the Woolly Rhino – muttered something about little nuisances who bumped into her and expected to be pulled out of her pond. Nevertheless she actually waded into the water, bent down and lifted the Woolly Rhino very gently in her mouth and deposited him on the bank.

'Now run off home before you catch cold,' said the Brontosaurus. 'And please do not bump into me again or I shall be most angry!'

The Woolly Rhino who felt and looked rather wet and foolish needed no further encouragement and, with his short, stubby tail between his legs, he set off homewards across the snow-covered plains.

After trudging through the deep snow the Woolly Rhino's fur became coated with tiny droplets of ice that sparkled as he walked and made him look very strange.

The snow became thinner on the ground as the Woolly Rhino continued on his way, and the temperature was slowly rising. By the time he came in sight of home, all the snow had disappeared and the sun was shining brightly!

Fly was sunning herself on the log when she heard footsteps approaching. She looked up and there was the Woolly Rhino.

'Woolly!' she gasped. 'Whatever has happened to you?'

'Never mind about that,' said the Woolly Rhino, for he had no intention of discussing his misadventures. 'What on earth has happened here? The snow has gone in and the sun is shining . . . Fancy that! And just when I was beginning to find my snow-hooves!'

'Never mind,' said Fly. 'The Woolly Mammoth will be back with winter again before too long.'

'Jolly good,' said the Woolly Rhino as he lay down to sunbathe. 'Jolly good!' And with that he fell fast asleep . . .